Anonymous

Coaquanock

A Song of Many Summers - In Four Cantos

Anonymous

Coaquanock
A Song of Many Summers - In Four Cantos

ISBN/EAN: 9783337269548

Printed in Europe, USA, Canada, Australia, Japan

Cover: Foto ©Andreas Hilbeck / pixelio.de

More available books at **www.hansebooks.com**

A Song of Many Summers.

IN FOUR CANTOS.

PHILADELPHIA:

The Germantown Social Publication Co.

MDCCCLXXVIII.

PRINTED BY
ALLEN, LANE & SCOTT,
233 South Fifth Street,
PHILADELPHIA.

To THOSE
WHOSE THOUGHTS
ARE WONT TO RETURN TO
THE THINGS THAT ONCE HAVE BEEN
IN OUR GOOD OLD TOWNS, WHOSE LEGEND-
ARY, TRADITIONAL, AND HISTORIC PECULIARITIES CLOTHE
THEM WITH THE MISTY AND MYSTERIOUS ATMOSPHERE OF THE
LONG PAST, AND WHOSE VARIED SCENES OF HILL, WOOD-
LAND, BATTLE-FIELD, AND BUSY MART, WITH
THEIR MANIFOLD SUGGESTIONS, HAVE
SO LARGELY CONTRIBUTED
TO THE MEMORIES
RECORDED
IN THESE PAGES,
ARE THEY RESPECTFULLY DEDICATED BY

THE AUTHOR.

PREFATORY NOTE.

THE characters introduced in this book (with one or two exceptions) are not fictitious, having been drawn, either from history or current allusion; while the legends and stories herein embraced have been obtained, for the most part, from repeated narration by early inhabitants, and are doubtless already familiar to many.

The Vocabulary of Indian terms at the end of the book explains the meaning of the words and names marked *.

CONTENTS.

COAQUANOCK.*

A SONG OF MANY SUMMERS.

" Would'st read thyself, and read thou knowest not what,
    And yet know whether thou art blest or not,
    By reading the same lines? O! then come hither
    And lay my book, thy head and heart together."

J. BUNYAN.

CANTO FIRST.

THE PIONEER.

THE PIONEER.

ONE morning—years how many since, 't would be
    A useless charge to task the memory—
Two travelers up the quiet street set forth
To seek the smiles of fortune farther north.
They were not poor, 't is true, nor yet in need
Of friends to cheer them in the town ; indeed,
So steadfast and fraternal were they all
In that good town, with its fair city hall,
Where all the weighty questions of the day,
First hither borne, re-echoed far away,
That she had earned a name afar and near
Which made her great men ever proud to hear—
" The good old village of Fraternal Love."
Yet, as each ship cast anchor in her cove—
From far left lands discharging plenteous store,
And bringing precious pilgrim freight once more,
Some restless dwellers of the place there were
Who ever sighed for less restricted air ;
These—as the bead the brim doth o'erpass,
Leave the more weighty malt to fill the glass ;
So while the flapping sails waved them adieu
From lofty yards still wet with last night's dew,
Our eager travelers left the narrow street,
And felt with joy God's soil beneath their feet.

But, oh ! what thoughts should we who tread to-day,
Heedless, those fields, now rich in corn and hay,

Awaken, could the scene, as it was then,
Re-picture its past loveliness again.
No axe had yet re-echoed up the vale,
Nor ruder hand within the sacred pale
Disturbed the tranquil age, than that of one
Whose brow betold the wild child of the sun ;
Here he, with freedom's boundary only drawn,
In triumph reveled from primeval dawn,
And with strung bow, and blade rough-hewn from stone,
Still reigned in peace, the white man scarce yet known.

With such a world spread round them to explore,
The two adventurers crossed the meadows o'er,
And soon were lost to view beneath the shade
That lay within the pine wood's sombre glade ;
No highway yet had linked the unborn town
With that fair sister destined to renown ;
No by-lane even marked the untrod way
Where speed so many busy souls to-day ;
The pathway then no stranger could descry,
Save he who bore the warrior's searching eye,
For wanton nature hid the hatchet's blow,
And stood her children's friend, the world's mute foe.
But he who now led first the tangled way,
No fear, nor doubt, nor hardships could dismay ;
A man of stalwart frame, but kindest brow,
Whose grave demeanor marked him, even now
In youth, as one who stood above the throng ;
Of royal blood he sprang, 't was said, but long
Had sought to fly the trammels of a life
Beset with fashion, envy, greed, and strife,
And with his lone companion thought to find,
Here in the virgin wood, some peace of mind.

They had thus journeyed on five miles or so,
To where the sloping lowlands 'gin to grow
More steep, to meet above those lovely hills
That fill, in springtime snows, the meadows' rills,
When, through some hapless turn, they lost the trail
(Which here bent northward over hill and dale),
And groping vainly round them for some sign,
Fatigued, at last, they sat them down to dine ;
And fain would they have lingered for awhile,
With sylvan dreams the noon hours to beguile ;
But bread had scarce restored their wearied strength,
When, through the deep wood shades, the tawny length
And visage of a stranger, hard, severe,
Strode forward, and unbidden, drew so near,
The startled feasters thought it most discreet
To grasp again their weapons at their feet.
But quite in vain their caution soon they learned
By one firm gesture, as the savage turned
And pointed eastward, where, at but a pace,
Were gathered six tall brothers of his race
In patient converse, guarding that red hand
With which the chieftain wields his dread command.
Defense, indeed, were needless, for the man
Who thus disturbed their peaceful meal began—
By that rude language which we may believe
Pere Adam first taught our fair mother Eve—
To welcome the intruders to this ground,
Where, hitherto, no pale-face rest had found.
Through signs he told them of his noble tribe
Who not yet knew that curse infernal—bribe.
He led them to a lofty spot near by,
Where naught was seen but boundless wood and sky,

Till far in hazy eastern distance shone
Those sand-spread shores then harborless and lone.
"All these are mine," he said, with sweeping hand;
Nor little dreamed he this unfenced land
Where he had roamed the hero from a boy—
Untried by art, dame nature's idle toy—
Should soon renounce his claim forever there,
And yield her prestige to a race more fair.

Yet in that scene to-day, behold the change !
Where many a wall and turret, new and strange,
Peep up to break this wandering dream of old,
And mock the shadowy past's dull tale, thrice told.
Time's finger e'er is rubbing, yet the trace
Of a good life it shall not all efface.

MAIDENHOOD.

THE LEGEND OF LOVER'S LEAP.

THE LEGEND OF WISSAHICKON.

MAIDENHOOD.

THE listless years have fled apace ;
    And now in mother's yearning face,
A bright-eyed daughter's beaming smile
Reflects, untainted yet with guile.
The maiden round her forest home
In happy childhood loves to roam,
For she no fairer heaven knows
Than this, to wander where repose
And rapture gild each halcyon day
With bliss, and keep the world away.
She loves that grove of hemlock trees
That sigh to every summer breeze ;
Or 'mid the vines that clothe the side
Of Wingohocking's* banks, to hide,
And watch the noonday shadows pass
Like phantom shapes adown the grass ;
But most of all she loves to be
With head bowed on a father's knee,
And hearken to the legends wild
And strange he's wont to tell the child,
While twilight lends her fairy charm,
And tints in colors soft and warm
The wainscots and the great wide stair
Out in the hall, till fancy there
Completes the wondrous pictures drawn
Of things and beings long since gone.

And one which pleased her more than all
Of these weird tales, we now recall :—

THE LEGEND OF LOVER'S LEAP.

IN this quiet glen, so lonely
  Now, where once 'twas bright and gay,
Peopled as it then was only
  By a race now passed away,
Stood long years ago, a wigwam—
  Nigh where that cliff rears to-day.

And aback those dreamy ages,
  Ere the pale-face scarred the way—
Dark-eyed maids and hoary sages
  Holding still unbounded sway—
Dwelt a chief there, brave and haughty,
  With a daughter fresh as May.

Charming was she as the river,
  Sparkling, dancing, as she came,
While around her lips a quiver
  Spake of love's yet slumb'ring flame,—
Though of this unruly passion
  Scarce she yet dared breathe the name.

But such doubts must have an ending;
  Lovers come as sure as years;
And like raindrops come they, blending
  With the rosebuds' smiles, sad tears;
And on this wise 'tis it happens,
  Youth's fond hopes oft change to fears.

Long the tender princess cherished
  Deep within her silent breast,
Thoughts upon her father's young braves ;
  And,—had she the truth confessed,
There was one alone among them
  To whom as naught seemed all the rest.

Fair was he, and like the chestnut,
  Fleet was he as the young deer,
Ardent was he as a lover
  Only can be, when—come near—
He a coquette's smile discovers,
  Where he fain would find a tear.

Long she listened to his wooing,
  While the sun fell down the sky ;
While the tide flowed soft beneath them,
  And the day went gently by :
While two nut-brown cheeks grew closer,
  When they thought none else were nigh.

Long she listened to his war-songs
  Of the Lenni Lenape,*
Of the great Five Nations' battles,
  Of the big Wapanachi.*
" People where the sun is rising "
  With their ancient pedigree.

Long she listened, nor aweary
  Grew she of those blissful hours,
Yet one sorrow in her heart lay—
  Like a weed among the flowers ;
Shading o'er love's perfect sunshine,
  Sapping sweetness from her showers.

First among her father's young men,
  Ere they stirred the council smoke ;
Ere the war-cry, " Petalamo auween,"*
  Through the sleeping woodlands broke,
Stood a brave of thirty summers ;
  Hard and strong he was as oak.

And 'twas he the sachem smiled on—
  Thought to take him for his son ;
Proud to wed unto his daughter
  " Man who many scalps had won ; "
But the maiden looked not on him ;
  All his glances she did shun.

Then the chieftain's brow was darkened ;
  Said he, " We the thing will test,
Whether in the slender sapling
  Or the oak shall be her nest ;
They shall run for her together,
  And she's his who runs the best."

Then long grew the hours and dreary,
  Ere that fatal dawn should break ;
Ere the fate of poor Wulisso*
  Should be destined at the stake !
And her heart waxed sick, for thinking
  One must suffer for her sake.

Thus, when evening breezes rustling,
  Lulled the forest leaves to sleep,
Softly whispered she, " Wulapan,*
  If I die, thou shalt not weep ;
For, when on thy lips grief murmurs,
  In thy heart my soul shall creep.

"And when wrapped in glittering wampum,*
  Resting low beneath the flowers,
Dancing onward in the spirit
  Happy as these noonday hours,
' While the leaves are raked above me '
  In the sap month—month of showers.

'' Thou shalt hear a sweet bird singing
  As thou goest on thy way,
And perchance thine arm may falter
  Ere thou fallest on thy prey.
Then, if thou shouldst hear ' Wischixi,'*
  Quick ! be strong, nor make delay.

'' But, if thou in doubt shouldst linger
  With thy tomahawk in air,
And thou hearest faint, ' Ekesa,'*
  Then thy foe's blood shalt thou spare ;
For where'er the hunt may lead thee,
  I shall still be with thee there.

"And I'll tell of Allowilek,*
  He who guards us all above ;
He who wipes away Suppinquall*
  From all eyes that weep for love ;
Elewussit,*—He the mighty,
  Yet as gentle as the dove.''

Thus, did poor Wulisso murmur
  In the gloaming eventide,
With the winking stars above her,
  With Wulapan at her side ;
He who, ere another sunset,
  Thought to win her for his bride.

Brightly broke the dawn that morrow
   O'er the rivals' measured ground,
Where, with many a tom and cymbal,
   Youths and women gathered round,
Fain to speed the fleet Wulapan,
   Runner with the fleetest hound.

But beyond the crowd of gazers,
   Nigh the painted trysting stake,
Waiting for the fatal moment
   When that warning cry should break
Like a death-song o'er her childhood—
   Sat Wulisso, for his sake.

Long there hung a deadly silence,
   Ere a shrill cry rent the air,
And two dark forms, like two roebucks,
   Darting from their hidden lair,
Upward flew amid wild whoopings,
   Breast to breast, with streaming hair.

For a moment drew Wulisso
   To the full her gentle height,
With her heart so wildly leaping,
   Cloudy visions dimmed her sight,
For it seemed as though Wulisso
   Yet might be a bride that night.

But, ere yet the goal they came near,
   By some daring hand unseen,
Like a snapped bow, lay Wulapan
   Low upon the trampled green ;
And Kschachan,* now the victor,
   Sought the princess, now his queen.

Sought Wulisso, aye ! but whither—
  One faint little cry uprose,
Where the big rock " Meechek achsink"*
  Stands there still in death's repose ;
" Ne Nipauwi,* one step nearer,
  And Wulisso ends her woes."

Quick ! Kschachan—darting toward her,
  Thought to seize her ere she fell ;
One dull plash adown the waters
  Echoed up the sunlit dell ;
Then, with measured pace advancing,
  Lone Wulapan said, " 'Tis well."

Slow he then drew nigh his rival,
  While a deep shade crossed his brow,
And with look of nameless anguish
  Murmured he, " 'Tis over now ;
Oh ! Kschachan, we are brothers,
  Can we raise the storm-wrecked bough ?

" Can we make flowers grow in winter,
  When we track the hungry deer ?
Can the heart give smiles of pleasure—
  When 'tis cold, and in the ear
A devil whispers ? Oh ! Kschachan,
  Can it ?   See ! our hands meet here."

On the cliff a sunbeam wavered ;
  Overhead the wild bird cried ;
" Hark ! she calls me," breathed Wulapan,
  Quick then, o'er the rock's steep side,
Down he plunged, nor made one murmur,
  For the brave had won his bride.

Among those braves that lingered still,
Yet loth to part from wood or hill,
With such fond life-long memories strewn,
Where worldly odds had ne'er been known,
Was one of more than common fame;
(Shickallemy was his name!)
Who came 'gainst each return of spring
His fruits of winter sports to bring,
And humbly bow before that door
Where he should reign a prince no more.
And at such times the little maid
Would oft draw nigh, nor was afraid
To clasp in her's his savage hand,
Nor by his half-bent form to stand
And count the beads that hung profuse
About his neck and belt and shoes.
And when he wandered round the place,
With sad forebodings on his face,
As each new step recalled to view
Some tree or haunt his old life knew,
The girl would lead to some quiet nook,
And there strive hard from out her book
To turn his thoughts from carnal things
To those which earnest study brings.
She'd tell him how his Manitou—
Her God—would some day life renew,
And make the birds and deer once more
As plenty as they were of yore.
(Though all this in her pupil's ear,
Wrought little comfort there, I fear;)
But once while they together sat,
Thus chatting o'er—now this, now that—
The child bethought her of an old
And wondrous tale her father told,

One time, about some neighboring ground,
Where once these Indian tribes had found
A happy home; so she began
Forthwith this tale to tell the man :—

THE LEGEND OF WISSAHICKON.

WHILE yet the Pale-face ne'er had peeped
    Within that tranquil vale,—where, steeped
In sombre, fir-clothed heights, and bound
On either side with moss-grown ground
And craggy cliff, a goodly stream
With many a rippling noontide gleam
Ne'er ceased her daily tithes to pay
To good Queen Ocean far away—
Deep sheltered from the hostile world,
The smoke from many a tent upcurled,
Where, round the wigwam fire, red dames
Talked o'er their tawny lords' brave names,
While they, with feathered death and bow
And trackless step, now quick, now slow,
Gave chase, in neighboring hills, the game,
There pasturing heedless, till death came
In one fell dart.   Life surely here—
With naught but Manitou to fear—
Seemed sweet to those blest sons of men ;
Yet it did find its cares e'en then,
For lo ! at last there came a day
Of sorrow and of dread dismay,
When from a lowering cloud that spread
Across the summer blue o'erhead,
Their God-chief's awful voice was heard,
As like the thunder rolled each word :—

" My children, I am called away
Where other souls my presence pray,

But ere I leave ye I must ask
One boon of all,—a simple task
'Twill be to those whose faith hath borne
The tests of fiery stake or thorn.
Yet some I know among ye who
Will find it hard to sin eschew
When left alone, and all must know,
An evil spirit dwells below
These rocks, and ever guards his chance
To tempt ye, with his fiendish dance
And wicked ways, to but forsake
My laws for aught that he may make ;
So, should he rise when I am gone,
Let no temptation lead ye on
To overstep the bounds here set
About your hunting-grounds, nor let
Aught of shape, however fair
And good it seems, entice ye where
My word hath said ye nay."

                     Thus said,
The cloudy spirit vanished
Into the air from whence it grew ;
And now a wide commotion flew
Throughout the warriors gathered there ;
And wondered all how soon, and where,
This new-brought ill its face should show,
To tempt their Eve-like hearts ; when lo !
Ere two short days had dragged away,
Within a distant wood, where lay
Soft twilight ever 'mong the trees,
Strange music stirred, and on the breeze
Of evening came wild shouts of mirth,
That seemed to wake the very earth,
So boisterous were they, and, alas !
The youths could not a moment pass

Till they with stealthy steps were brought
Close to that God-forbidden spot ;
And there, as o'er a lofty brow
That hemmed the darksome glade, they now
Did creep, behold ! a wondrous sight,
Such as their souls' most fancied flight
Had ne'er conceived of, met their eyes,
Even like some glimpse of paradise.
A Pale-face spirit, lank and grim,
With horns and claws that gave to him
A weird, unearthly look, sat high
Upon a rock that towered nigh ;
And while below fair damsels played
Wild antics through the woodland shade,
He to loud fits of mirth gave vent,
As near the maidens came and went,
And cast before him laurels wreathed
In crowns ; then—ere the watchers breathed,
Lest they should be discovered there—
Lo ! quick as lightning 'thwart the air,
The fiendish god turned full to view,
And, ere the astonished gazers knew,
Close by their side, with devilish smile
He stood, and thus addressed them, while
With spell-bound gaze—their eyes made dim
With fascination—now from him
From whom they had no power to go,
Did wander to the scene below,
Where still,—though now the sun had gone—
To music soft, the dance went on :—

" Wouldst thou, oh man, to pleasure blind,
Seeking a gift thou ne'er shalt find,

Led by a promise far astray
Along that hard and narrow way,
Wouldst thou no more sad anguish know,
Nor lose the chase with feeble bow?
Wouldst thou be free, and tread once more
The grounds your fathers roamed of yore?
Wouldst thou find game in every copse
And stream, and gather plenteous crops
In autumn, yet know naught of care
Nor labor, but with damsels fair
And waxen pass life's endless days
Along my smooth and flower-girt ways?
Wouldst thou, in fine, the height of bliss
Attain?   I offer ye all this,
And more ; come, follow me.''

                                        He ceased,
And, like some semi-human beast,
His bloodcast eye the crowd scanned o'er,
Where some, entranced, could hear no more,
But, weak of heart, with outstretched hand,
Forgetting quite their God's command
Of yester morn, were quickly led
Adown the cliff with dizzy head
And burning brain, and those, alas !
From mortal view for aye did pass ;

But some there were who still delayed,
Not resolute, and half afraid
To follow ; lingering there they stood
Till lo ! the dawn crept through the wood ;
And on its gentle face, behold !
A strange-shaped cloud, fringed round with gold,
Came darkly flitting through the sky,
Till seemingly it had drawn nigh

Above that gathering in the vale.
Then quick the subtle fiend turned pale,
As from the frowning mists o'erhead
A mighty voice and angry said :—

" Depart, ye tempter of the night !
Hence ! Dare ye show your face in light ?
Did I not bid thee well beware
Lest thou shouldst fall in thine own snare ?"

The spirit fled, but scarce had left
His seat, when some great earthquake cleft
The rock beneath his feet in twain,
And deep he plunged between.   In vain
He strove to rise again, for quick
The waters from a hillside creek
O'er-ran that pool, that marks to-day
The spot where Satan passed away.
Then kindly smiled the Manitou
On those around, and said :—

　　　　　　　　　　　" To you
My children, who have yet withstood
The things of evil for the good ;
To you, whose faith has ne'er been turned
Astray by sin, well have ye earned
The joys foretold ; so now go forth ;
The boundless woods from south to north,
From east to west, are yours to roam
For aye, till I shall call ye home."

The sachem lent attentive ear,
This legend old again to hear ;

But when the child had ceased, he laid
His rough, red hand on hers and said :—
"The pale-face child is good ; she loves
To talk of happy things, like doves
That mourn in the tall pines near by,
Where some loved things did chance to die.
The pale-face child speaks well, but she
Must not seek fruit on the forest tree ;
That hunting-ground at the setting sun,
Where each brave goes when the race is won,
Is not the white man's paradise,
To which, from earth, he hopes to rise.
We cannot think this, child, oh, no !
But see ! the day dies, I must go. '

Yet ere they stirred he took a ring
From off his hand, and put the thing,
Set 'round with many a glittering stone,
In the maiden's lap.
      "When thou hast grown
To be a woman, wise and fair,"
He said, "then, in thy twilight prayer,
Thou'lt think of him who, long ago,
Did give thee this ; and when the snow
Lies deep o'er two lone graves, why then
We'll know if we shall meet again."

The girl bent down her head in tears,
While the cricket chirped in her listless ears,
And when she rose to speak at last,
The chief from her side for aye had passed.

CANTO THIRD.

THE

HATCHET UNEARTHED.

A TALE OF '76.

THE HATCHET UNEARTHED.

AGAIN the sceptred hand of time
Hath waved the flight of years,
And now that face of springtime smiles
Is steeped in autumn tears.

The child who sought a mother's love
Hath won a mother's cares ;
The sunshine dress of life's fair morn
A twilight shadow bears.

But ere the resting day hath broke,
Lo ! through the dawn's thick gloom
There comes a sound all earth to rouse,
Hark ! 'tis the cannon's boom.

And through the weary, sleepless hours,
Come echoing from afar,
O'er fields that birds once rang with mirth
The groans, the din of war.

Then, bending o'er a mother's breast,
A few hard, hot tears fall ;
A few fond words of love are passed,
Of faith, and—that is all.

" I came not to bring peace on earth,
No, not peace, but a sword ;
To make a household friend a foe,"
Thus spake our blessed Lord.

The swelling, pent up sense of right,
　That slumbers through the land,
From myriad hearts bursts forth, with might
　That wrong cannot withstand.

And if the trials of defeat
　Give test of faith and blood,
They can but stay the germ of bloom
　That crouches in the bud.

At length our day of horror dawns;
　The sun withholds her light,
Ashamed to pierce the dankish veil
　That shrouds the woeful sight,

Where man and beast together blend
　A ghastly, trickling flow:
The grim attest of loyalty,
　Whose price but God can know.

And while an anguished mother strains
　Each parting step to hear,
A boy gone forth, his boyhood's yoke
　Hath cast in one last tear.

But ere the roll of honor claims
　His name—her sacrifice—
One love there is, that in his heart,
　Next to a mother's lies.

A maiden's, 'tis, whose love-flushed cheek
　And kindling eyes control
The young man's heart with magic will,
　Enrapturing his soul.

Thither, with faltering step, he tends,
  And, kneeling to those eyes,
Begs one last boon, than which to him
  Earth hath no richer prize.

When fair Pandora, tempted, touched
  The spring, her box flew ope,
And every blessing hidden there
  Escaped but one—'twas Hope.

Alas ! fond youth, alas ! fair maid,
  That blessing staid for you ;
A cherished jewel still to be,
  To cheer life's journey through.

The maiden gave the precious thing,
  And with it, too, she sealed
That impress which man cannot lose,
  E'en on the battle-field.

But swallowed in the engulfing tide
  Are all those placid dreams
Of youth and love, like thoughts at sea
  Of far-off mountain streams.

With softened voice the captain cries
  (While death her thunder rolls,
And one by one her victims takes),
  " Pray, comrades, for your souls."

And lost forever is the name
  The village won of yore ;
Her peaceful homes are battle-grounds,
  Her floors are stained with gore.

The kine that pastured on her lawns
    Are seized by famished men,
And torn as vultures tear their prey,
    In some sequestered glen.

But not enough, the sick'ning deeds
    That stain war's boiling tide ;
Her pomp and boast—her white cockades—
    Flaunt high on every side.

Yet strife, thank God, can't last for aye,
    The battle's lost or won ;
The storm that roughs the midnight sea
    Is calmed in morning sun.

The shades of sorrow may endure
    Where night her mantle throws,
But joy still ushers in the morn,
    And banishes our woes.

And as, when first the storm hath passed,
    And earth is bathed in gold,
The distant East still murmurs o'er
    Her tale of ruin told,

So now, ere yet the peace-stacked arms
    Stand rusting in the shield,
The voices of tradition tell
    The wounds which time hath healed.

A TALE OF '76.

IN the quaintest old house, on a quaint old street
   In our town, dwells a quaint old dame, so sweet
That no one dare credit her statement at all,
That when this world claimed her, "she came with a call."
Now "a call," we believe, is,—at least, so 'tis said,—
An office by Satan conferred on the head
Of a babe from birth gifted with vision so rare
That it may see wonders, where we see but air.
And long hath it been the world's wont to believe
That strange woman nature, e'en from *Mater* Eve,
Hath ever been chosen the fittest of tools
To aid the dark fates to turn men into fools.
And those who (with this evil penchant endowed)
Are doomed on a broomstick to o'er-ride the cloud,
Have pledged to renounce in red writing of blood,
Every duty a Christian may owe to his God ;
And branded and known by their coarse, wrinkled face,
Hairy lip, furrowed brow, and a sickly grimace ;
With a dog and a spindle their sole bosom chums,
On their odious journey they go, with bent thumbs,
From the fumes of Gehenna slow stealing their way,
With wild chant, while stars wink at the fast fading day ;
Now striving to tell, from the wisdom-bird's flight,
The dark deeds afloat on the wings of the night ;
Or summoning woe, it may hap, on the head
Of some innocent victim whose steps they've misled ;
Or oftener calling on Æolus' breath
To blast some doomed crop, or inflict pain or death ;

Or make barren the fruitful ; with all powers, in fine,
Like gods, e'en themselves, everything to divine,
Save one—their own fate ; for—whatever their charm,
Themselves, it is said, they can ne'er save from harm.

Be this as it may, then, of one thing be sure,
That the likes of this creature so strangely demure,
Should never have fallen to duties so base ;
But one look at the hard lines that hung round that face,
And the keen eyes beneath them, that flashed with wild fire,
Filled the stranger with doubt, when he fain would admire.

Well ! thus it did happen, a fair lady came
One day to the door of this fay-gifted dame,
And straightway besought her to make no delay,
But forthwith to tell her, if she could well say
What the drift of the future should be ; for, alas !
She had had woeful fears of what might come to pass ;
Nor had slept oft of late, for some phantoms unknown
That around her night slumbers dread horrors had thrown.
Then, with her thumb-finger drawn up to her eye
That fell to the hearthstone, the crone made reply :—

> " If the maiden fain would know
> What awaits her here below,
> Why her wonted slumbers light
> Are beset, the livelong night,
> With those strange, uncanny things
> Youth's quick budding ever brings,
> I must know, ere I begin,
> Both her name, her hame, and kin.
> Yea, and she should tell me, too,
> What she dreamed last night, and who

First she met when from the door
She came hither, rich or poor,
Man or beast ; I must know all,
Even to the *first foot* fall,
Ere I tell the future's call."

Then spoke the fair maiden, " Good dame, you well know
An old-fashioned mansion some two miles below
On the highway, stands close by the greenery path ?
A wood rail round the front, skirt with tall trees, it hath,
And a garden behind where the old-fashioned rose,
'Mid a bower of fox-grape and columbine, blows.
'T was here, so 'tis said, on one bright April morn,
Just twenty years gone, e'en to day, I was born ;
And now, since you know well the place whence I came,
I'm sure 'twill be idle to tell you my name ;
So list to my story.   Some ten years ago,
Long ere these fair hills were made foul with man's woe ;
When each hour seemed a sun-spot along youth's smooth way,
And each morrow brought pleasures undreamed of to-day,
There came to our door a plain, gloomy-faced child,
Whose looks told a weary tale, e'en when she smiled,
And said she had journeyed, with feet bruised and sore,
O'er many a mile, nor once paused, till our door
She had gained.   Having heard long ago, when at home,
Of my father's kind name, she had made bold to come
And beseech him to hire her, for good or for ill,
As servant or slave, or what place she might fill,
Where 'mong good kind folk she might wander no more,
But earn her own bread, for, indeed, she was poor.

My father, reluctant, assented at last
To these pleadings to shelter the hapless outcast.

But the child had not been in the house for one week,
E'er she proved far too worthy the place she did seek ;
And, indeed, life grew easy, with one at my side
To whom all my cares I could safely confide ;
Yet not her good labors alone did I prize ;
The servant soon grew to a friend in rough guise,
And, unlike other girls of her years and her station,
She was gifted by nature with a keen revelation
Of beauty inherent in meadow and wood,
Like the dream, which the dreamer alone understood ;
And oft at the verge of the hedge she would stand,
With her pale face bent skyward, her hoe in her hand,
While—listing some bells far-off murmuring chime,
Her thoughts to wild fancies of cloudland would climb.
But she loved most to forecast, when we sauntered alone,
What great things I should do when to woman I'd grown ;
And still, 'mongst these fanciful dreams which she drew,
Was she wont long to dwell on one thing which she knew
Was, ere long, to befall our own home ; a sad day
Should soon come when death's searching hand fate should
    weigh
O'er that once peaceful house ; yet, when all this had past,
My destiny surely 't would be, at the last,
To wed a young soldier, as handsome as brave,
Whose life, at the risk of my own, I should save.
Thus she foretold, and with such wild thoughts did beguile
Youth's long days,—as good company shortens each mile.

But those bright years soon fled, and the dark years began,
And off with those blest years my gay childhood ran ;
While thro' the hushed mornings came echoes of war
To bury loved silence in death's maddening roar.

And, while we were absent a few days in town,
And the maid was left there in the mansion alone,
The enemy coming, marched into the place,
And the poor girl too soon, with a woe-begone face,
Became hostess and servant to mark and obey
What e'er her new guest—a young major—might say.
And here for a week, filled with shame for her fate,
The return of her folk from the town she did wait,
Still thinking perchance, as the conflict came nigh,
. That these guests so unwelcome would soon need to fly.
And when, one dark day, in the garden she stood,
While bullets came thick from a neighboring wood,
The soldier called out to her well to have care
Of the shot that flew hither and yon through the air,
Lest some half-spent ball should find rest in her head,
And make her a grave on her own garden-bed—
She gave him no heed, but well guarded her chance
To escape to the foe that now fast made advance,
' Till soon her late guest put quick sheath to his sword,
And that night the old mansion to us was restored.
We returned, nothing loth, and the brave wench shed tears
At our coming. Then gone were my doubtings and fears.
Yet now, with an ill-concealed look of her own,
Would Justina still prate of the young major gone,
While her face well betrayed a sad lingering there,
Of a sense which too often youth's heart fails to share ;
And I too grew curious sometime to see
This stranger, though enemy still he might be.

Day crept on day till my patience grew frail,
Lest this prophetess mine, with her bodings, might fail.
Then at last, one sad eve, when the land far and near
Re-echoed with moanings that filled all with fear,

Came a pale, speechless cluster of men to the door,
While on a rude stretcher a wrapt form they bore,
Which down on the floor in the parlor they laid,
And bid me quick sop the red stains from his head.
Then, while I scarce knew what dark task now was mine,
Justina brought water to bathe him, and wine
To revive him, but when her eyes fell on that face,
Of the blood in her cheeks there quick fled every trace;
As she cried, 'My poor major, 'tis he,' then adown
By his side, did she wipe his white brow with her gown.
Then in came the surgeon, and men gathered round,
While through the dark room hung a silence profound,
As he told to us all the sad close soon to come,
When the soldier should list to his last reveille drum.

He died there; and with that due pomp of sad war,
To a neighboring churchyard the body they bore,
While with a sick heart, at the horrible sight
I had witnessed, I fled to my room for the night.
But sleep was not mine, for the black haunting thought
That the death of the soldier, and the maid's strange words
    brought,
Returned o'er and o'er, 'till my head seemed aflame
With a dream for whose pictures I've ne'er found a name.
And now listen! that night, as I knelt down in prayer,
A hand was laid cold on my loose flowing hair,
And turning I saw, bent low, close to my breast,
The face and the head that I that day had drest.
Then a voice came, 'Oh! lady! weep not, nor lament
That the sum of my life with this quick close is spent.
This same morn, on the field, in the thick of the fight,
When man breast to man, each contended the right,

My sword o'er the life of a fair youth hung nigh ;
But see ! by one look it was stayed ! you ask why ?
Ah ! tell me, dost thou know the ways of the heart ?
Or canst thou tell whither it flings its keen dart ?
Go seek the wide world through, perchance thou shalt find
Some true heart, that shall pierce thee with love.   Ah ! too
    kind
Was my own, in arresting my hand from that blow,
By the weight of another, dear bought I my foe.
But hark you, the life this day spared by my own,
Lives for some good ; for thee ! aye ! though each yet un-
    known.'
The voice ceased ; I fell back as the form left my sight,
Yet e'en now the sad look that he gave me that night,
Like a spectre comes oft through the late twilight gloom,
And stares at me where'er I turn in my room,
And Justina but wanders with sad, downcast eye
Through the house, while my questions receive no reply.

Thus ends my dark story, good dame, and if thou
Canst divine aught of hope in it, tell me it now.''

A long pause ensued ere the weird crone then said,
With a quiet, indifferent turn of the head : —

     ''Fear not, lady, what has past,
     In a mould thy fate is cast,
     Wouldst thou change it for another?
     Shall a girl disown her mother?
     Thou hast yet the man to meet
     Who those arching lips shall greet ;
     Under that same mystic ring
     Round your ceiling there circling,

Where beneath, a blood-stained floor
Tells a soldier is no more,
Thou a wedding-ring shall take,
And thy life-long vow there make,
To never more thy love forsake.

But ere that day thy house shall be
Bereft of mortal tenancy :
Dust shall hang upon her walls,
Haunting echoes thrill her halls ;
All that once wrought comfort there
Shall be stripped and dank and bare.
But when the spooks have had their day ;
.When the dead man rots in clay;
When the tug of war hath ceased ;
When grim death hath had her feast ;
When these things have come to pass,
And mounds now brown are green with grass,
And thou hast o'er-reached hope,—why, then,
Thou'lt do well to seek me again.''

The woman ceased, and from her rigid face,
But not so cronish, vanished every trace
Of superstition, as, with heartfelt shake
Of hands, the maiden now her leave did take.
*   *   *   *   *   *   *   *

A month had passed : the house again
Was girt without by armed men,
Who waited there from morn till night
Some chance to meet their foe in fight.
For now, within those fast-barred doors
Primed weapons strewed the barren floors.
Besieged it was ; but who within
'Gainst such great odds dare think to win?
Yet three lone souls, for one whole day,
Had kept the enemy at bay.

A gallant youth, whose glittering dress
Appeared some high rank to express ;
A lady, pale, but with flushed cheek
That mingling hope and fright did speak ;
And by her side a comely maid,
Whom neither hope nor fear dismayed.
These, weak of hand, of heart but bold,
Like stalwart knights in tower of old,
Each stationed with a duty set ;
Unmoved by aught of outward threat,
Defied, unscathed, the maddening throng,
Of those who fain would do them wrcng.

But ill-matched strife soon comes to end,
Whate'er man's prowess to defend.
Within that triple heart-bound ring
There rose a moment's questioning :
The loathsome hour had come anigh
When one must go or all must die ;
Some herald brave at once must pierce
The ranks of those besiegers fierce,
And haste to summon friendly aid,
That, long expected, still delayed.
But who should take the fatal task,
Each could not venture each to ask.
To leave two helpless women there,
Of course, the soldier could not dare ;
And though he fain would send the maid,
And had the gentle lady stayed
To share his fate for weal or woe,
Good judgment would not have it so.
Besides, Justina (for 'twas she
That was the helpmeet of the three)

Was better fitted to the place,
The sight of shot and fire to face :
So thus, at last, they did decide,
To deck the lady that eve tide,
In some deft military guise
That should awaken no surprise ;
And from the window let her down,
Whence she might haste to the distant town ;
Well trusting to her faithful heart
To bid her do her chosen part,
And to her guileless look and sweet,
If she a sentinel might meet ;

Thus, as the dusk of evening fell,
The damsel, clad in wrappings well,
Did, even as they first did plan,
A moment the dark landscape scan ;
Then from the window softly creep,
Speed fast adown the orchard's steep,
And thro' the outposts near thus pass,
With feet that scarcely tipped the grass,
While sleeping moonbeams shone to view
A thing so like them, none scarce knew
The shape that quick came flitting by
The camp, till she unwittingly
Stepped o'er a stile, where, at his post
A picket hailed the lovely ghost,
As erst he deemed she was ; but when
She paused, through mist around the fen
That barred the path, to pick her way,
The sentinel thought her flight to stay—
Yet still did doubt, as from the shade
The figure 'neath a moonbeam strayed ;

Nor did he well know how to bring
To halt, this speechless, doubtful thing,
Till, with a backward flinging glance,
Far o'er the meadow, he 'held her dance,
And, ere his weapon thought to seize,
Had lost her 'mong the darksome trees.

That night, ere morrow's dawn awoke,
Loud shouts athwart the village broke,
And wide-spread voices stirred the air
With mingled triumph and despair,
As dashing up the highway came,
With jaded steed and sword aflame,
All spattered o'er with foam and grime,
Those gallant men, who, in good time
From one had learned the pending fate
That did their chief, her friend, await.
And in the van of that hot throng
That now the wild crowd pressed along,
Till to the walls they were brought nigh
Of the old house, came one whose eye—
All gentle though it was—dispelled,
Where'er it lit, all doubt, that held
An upraised hand, as through the fray
On foot, the maid now pressed her way,
As erst, 'mong Saragoza's dead,
Her dark maid stalked with fearless tread,
Now leading on the sallying host,
Now filling some new vacant post,
Or now with gentle female grace
Appeasing death on some drawn face.
The tears, the blood that that morn shed
In heaven alone are numbered.

But ere the sun brought close of day,
And on the field his last gleams lay,
Forgot was all the morning's strife ;
Such is this tossing tide of life !
That now hurls down some cavern dark,
While on its breast the trembling ark
Of hope stares at destruction, when,
Lo ! into sunlit meads again
It quickly glides, where birds and flowers
Soon veil the thoughts of darker hours.

So now to those two souls it seemed,
Who down the garden pathway dreamed;
While birds, in tranquil skies o'erhead,
But mocked the hapless morning's dead ;
Nor thought they aught of evil passed,
But of this new-brought joy at last,
For, 'mid the tested hearts that day,
Two promised to be one for aye.

*   *   *   *   *   *   *   *   *

Ten summers more had suckled, nursed, and died ;
Ten more posthumous chill-born winters sighed
Amid the trees and down the village street,
And searched the shelving eaves with driving sleet ;
And with pale, fleecy hands had deftly crowned,
With heaven-wrought wreathes, the greening soldiers' mound ;
And now—as spring again, 'mid flowers and grass
Came forth, a lady up the street did pass,
While round her face a smile of pleasure gleamed,
That all things now so fair and happy seemed ;
For at her side, e'en like the playful spring,
There danced a blue-eyed, guileless little thing

That more than paid for those short years of care,
Its life had cost two patient hearts to share.
Yet still, beneath that smile of present joy,
There crept some shadow of the past's alloy ;
As on that latch she laid her hand once more,
Where she strange truth had learned in days of yore.

Across the shadowy floor, as she went in,
There sat, naught changed,—save grown perhaps more thin
And wrinkled, marking thus the years since flown,—
The same sweet smiling, half-mysterious crone.
She gave her guest good welcome, and then sought
To know the changeful things the years had brought,
Or if those castles fair youth erst did build
Were crumbled yet ; if aught had been fulfilled
Of all she once had made bold to forecast,
If fact, in truth, had outrun hope at last.
The lady told her tale, e'en as it had been,
Nor failed to note the joys 'twas hers to win
Through all life's cares ; but when she came to tell
A wondrous thing that had that morn befell,
While yet in gray of dawning, at the gate,
The figure of Justina (who of late
Had been on some good service in the town)
Appeared with pallid look and eyes cast down ;
And stood and waved thrice, gently with her hand,
As if to bid adieu her much-loved land ;
And thrice turned back her head, then passed away,
As through the trellis broke the beams of day ;
The woman's face more troubled grew and wan,
And when the lady ceased she thus began :—

> "In the gloaming skies I see
> Visions of futurity ;

There on yonder grass-green lawn,
Images of things agone.
And on every foggy night,
Like the morn of that dread fight
When the tories took the town,
Ride three horsemen up and down—
Across the green and 'round yon trees,
And bare their shorn necks to the breeze ;
While each man dangles at his hilt
His head, that tells of blood long spilt.
And thus is kept my memory green
Of those who can no more be seen.
Aye ! thus we know, too, e'er we see,
Things where we ken they should not be ;
Now seeming like some real thing there,
Now melting into viewless air ;
That since the spirit life hath fled,
The body e'er it lies, is dead.
The good Justina is no more.
At that same misty, dawning hour
When last thou sawest her shape this morn,
To her new home had she been borne ;
To thee I'll pledge my soul this night,
My lady, if I prove not right."

The matron now brushed one stray tear aside,
As in the good dame's hand her hand did bide
A moment, as she left some token there,
For all the oft-told truths she'd come to hear.
And as adown the street once more she went,
While on her child her loving eyes now bent,
Fresh tears would uprise, as fond memories brought
Back from the past full many a long-hushed thought ;•
And drew upon the shimmering spring-time air,
The shapes of things, alas ! no longer there.
'Twas as this woman strange, but now had said,
The spirit stays e'en where the form is dead.

That night, when drew the coach up to the door,
The good spouse on his brow some shadow bore,
As forward ran two little pattering feet,
Ere the child was raised a father's lips to meet;
And as now, toward them both a sweet face drew,
Hopeful, yet sad, they all more silent grew;
While each did seem to read in each that word
That chilleth mortal heart where'er 'tis heard.
Death, erst a stranger, yet a guest to be,
Whom all must welcome give, full cheerfully,
How e'er he comes, or loathsome or mild-eyed,
Who, where he comes forever there must bide,
Had that morn, gently drawn from mortal gaze
That faithful girl, who in her by-gone days,
With toiling hands that many a comfort wrought,
And words of hope when hope had come to naught,
A bright track left across life's studded sky,—
A trail whose light still lingered in the eye.

And now, as night dews gently settled down
Upon the woods, and o'er the drowsy town,
Far up the hill, against the pale eve's light,
The parting stage, low, rumbling, passed from sight;
Then toward the house the silent gathering drew,
And thence they now must vanish from our view.

THE CALUMET OF PEACE.

THE CALUMET OF PEACE.

OH, Time, hard father, man to thee
    Must still bend low the filial knee.
A thousand years in thy vast sight,
When past, are brief as watch of night;
And all the changes thou hast wrought
Mark but the onward growth of thought;
The cell from which the world began,
And blossomed forth in birth of man;
Her fruits that multiply with years,
And shower knowledge—though with tears;
The ceaseless flowing of the brook;
They all are noted in thy book,
As the brief doings of a day
Of whose long morrow, who shall say?

Then what are these few score of years,—
Fed with some smiles, quaffed more with tears,—
Since brave hearts sowed with blood the fields
Where freedom now her harvest yields?
What all the leaping joys that thrill
The heart of youth, or what the chill
That too soon follows, as the dew
That creeps on daylight's loveliest hue?
Or what the grave, where lost ones sleep
Unmindful, though veiled virgins weep?
The fluttering choir where youth and maid
From Psalms to thoughts of love are strayed?
Or flower-decked altar where they bow,
While soft winds heavenward bear their vow?

Lo ! these to thee are but as sands that spread
Egyptian deserts, or the ocean's bed ;
Or e'en as pale Vesuvian ashes borne
From Naples' night, to dark Phœnicia's morn.
Empyrean winged, a deadly shade they cast
Too oft beneath where'er their flight hath passed.
Awhile we blossom as the bridal rose,
Awhile we bear, then fade in death's repose.

From midnight suns that glare the northern sky,
Or paint Norwegian hills in crimson dye,
To Afric's depths, where nature's bosom teems
With life that feeds upon her while she dreams ;
From studious winter, hoary bearded o'er,
To jocund spring that opes love's heart once more ;
From flower-crowned summer's sated basking brow,
To fruitful autumn, with her laden bough
Replete with every mortal need—and then,
Still on to winter's pallid frown again,
Thy 'during eye a heartless vigil keeps,
Nor resteth ever, nor for any weeps.
Unlike that world that echoes smiles again,
Thou, marble-visaged, scorn'st the smiles of men.

————————

Full many a turn thou now may'st trace
On father Chronos' dialed face ;
Full many a change, too, mayest thou see
On earth ; yet this long mystery
Thou durst not probe, but still look on,
And note and learn from things agone.

Here through the town those years ago,
The ox, o'er grass-grown clods, full slow,
His way did take, and on his back
Did bear the heavy-laden sack
Unto the mill, that stood just there
Where now those brown-stone fronts appear,
And from its clumsy timbered wheel
Did shake the lazy drops, and steal
The idle mill-stream's dormant power,
Converting thus the grain to flour.

Here where the shorn lawn sweeps, close by,
A mill-pond mirrored back the sky ;
Nor little did the miller ken
The unborn force that, even then,
Within those placid waters lay,
Awaiting yet man's dawning day ;
But there, content to plod on still,
The years went, even as the mill.
Three times a week the lumb'ring coach
Did wake the town with its approach,
And drop, perchance, some stranger down,
Or spread fresh news i' the sleepy town.
But lo ! where are those toilers now
Who earned hard bread with beaded brow ?
A finger's touch, a whisper's breath
Hath spanned the earth ; yea, even death
Must leave life's 'during voice behind,
Within some phantom wheel confined.

But what avail to thus prolong
The numbers of my idle song.

The days still come, the years still go,
Full fast to some, to some but slow;
The rose still blooms, the leaf still falls,
And the brook through endless childhood crawls;
The heart of man still stoops to sin,
Yet thinketh still to enter in
Where few shall be, and prays and yearns—
But still with carnal passions burns;
The youth still pleads the court of Jove
To tune all harsher things to love,
Yet with drawn bow and quivering aim,
Still sighteth he thy throne, O fame!
And what the end?   All else may die;
The day, the night—yea, earth and sky
May melt in chaos! but the soul,—
A thing the fates alone control;
All joy, all sorrow nourished there,
Yet shapeless and unseen as air,—
Shall wake, and sleep, then wake again,
To realms well kept from mortal ken.

VOCABULARY

OF

PENNSYLVANIA INDIAN TERMS.

Manayunk, *place of drinking;* Schuylkill, *noisy stream;* Tulpehocken, *land of turtles.*